KB096961

"미소의 기적" 외

수필

# Miraculous Smile and Other Writings

**초판 1쇄 발행일** 2017년 4월 25일

**지은이_** 김학진
**펴낸이_** 김동명
**펴낸곳_** 도서출판 창조와 지식
**디자인_** (주)북모아
**인쇄처_** (주)북모아

**출판등록번호_** 제2015-000037호
**주소_** 서울시 성수동 성수이로18길 31, 103호(성수동2가, 풍림테크원)
**전화_** 1644-1814
**팩스_** 02-2275-8577

ISBN 979-11-6003-045-7  03800

지식의 가치를 창조하는 도서출판 **창조와 지식**
www.mybookmake.com

진솔하고 쉬운 언어가 순수하게 다가오는 영어 에세이 모음

# Miraculous Smile
## and
## Other Writings

HakJin Kim

# ■ CONTENTS

Introduction

A Mother's Job                          09

A Beauty                                13

Children's Day of 2016                  17

A Woman's Triumph                       22

Miraculous Smile                        26

Chocolate                               31

Precious Moments in Buenos Aires        37

Memories of Living in America           44

Truth                                   55

Marriage                                60

Green                                   68

At My Age                               73

The Wrong Direction                     80

On the Bus                              86

One morning in January last year, I woke up feeling the ripple of my late mother's sweet smile she gave me in the dream. She looked so real that I couldn't think of her as dead. By the time I got up for the day, I could decide that I would release myself from grief that had lasted for months. Her smile helped me presume that she was doing well in the other world and also seemed to encourage me to record some things residing in my mind. Since then I tried to keep past memories about my mother in my notebook and began to make an attempt to write essay reviews.

As I had enjoyed excellent essays written by American writers in The Best American Essays, a yearly book, for years, I could experience a variety of higher state of consciousness that led me to leave short reviews. And then I kept writing and ended my stories up to fourteen. Most of my writings are only two or three pages long, but I can be sure I implied what was going through my mind. This year is special because I reach the age of sixty, so I take courage to have my personal writings published. Perhaps publishing this trivial stuff would be a bold attempt in light of my writing experience, especially in English since I only wrote term papers for grades and thesis to achieve my master's degree when I was in the United States. But I'm going to step out of my apprehension decisively before it's too late. Now I hope that this exciting departure will make the road to my future career to be a writer. I thank some friends of mine and my family for warm support.

HakJin Kim
March 6, 2017

# A Mother's Job

We were in the middle of the crowd, walking around a traditional market with our arms folded to get some stuff for lunch. Groceries seemed to follow us because we were blocked on each step by market people who were thrusting their goods right under our noses. And at last my mother turned her face to me and declared she would make kimchi fried rice at home. She looked so young that she seemed to be in her forties. On grinning back at her, I faced the reality that she had gone to the other world. For some time lying in bed I meditated what happened in my dream missing my mother whose life had been always towards me like a sunflower. She was my guardian angel at home even though I didn't ask her to be, so she'd been ready to meet my any request at any time.

As I thought of my mother's action, I wondered how she could show up like this in my dream. She might want to show what she could do for me after she hadn't been with me in this world since last August. The market along with her suggestion of making some food wasn't the scene I'd ever imagined. Just lately my mind has hovered the panoramic scenes related my late parents, particularly my mother who had lived alone for about seventeen years after my father's death in 1999. Although she had been in grief over the loss of her husband, she never neglected to make food for me to let me take out every week. I should have shown my gratitude to her dedication, but I didn't do it because I thought she did her job as it was.

She was born to be a devoted mother. She was always busy at home to feed me and my brothers. She had never tired in doing her job. Especially she knew that I was fastidious about food. And she couldn't let it go like that. When I would like to skip the meal, my mother slid into the kitchen in the middle of dinner without a word to make another dish to have me eat. As a mere child at that time, I thought it was just the way my mother treated me all the time. This warm-hearted manner had lasted until she died of cancer last summer. As a woman in my late 50s as well as a lonely daughter without mother, I began to consider the meaning of motherhood.

My job as a mother was to feed, educate and try to make him a capable man, not focusing on giving delicious food. For my ambition I pushed my son ahead to make him be bright and capable regardless of what food he liked. Speaking of favorite food, I happen to know he loves tobu recently. But my mother was the opposite. She didn't care about my grade reports because she always trusted in me, and her job was solely to cook food to please her children. She had been in the kitchen for the most part of her life for mealtimes. So my brothers and I never had a feeling of lack and grew well like trees soaking nutrition.

One of my precious memories with my mother reminds me of what my mother's job was to be. One day in my college days I ran away from home because I had a big argument with my father who was so intimate that he liked to meddle in everything I did. As soon as I shut the door behind me, I found myself that there was nowhere to stay that night. I had to go back home late that day. The doorbell rang and the door was open in a second by my mother who seemed to wait for me at the door. She looked at me in the eyes, said nothing, and began to set the table with my favorite food. I was led to the dining room and being watched while eating. After I finished my meal, she went to bed confirming her job done with satisfaction.

January 26, 2016

# A Beauty

One Thursday afternoon in spring 2016, I sat in on a figure croquis class, a six month course at Sungnam Art Center. I've been interested in sketching things since long before. In class I watched how participants described a naked model who kept changing poses every three minutes. While the instructor just looked around each work commenting and correcting lines and touches, I was looking at works done by an acquaintance that seemed to express every moment with all her heart and soul. I marveled at how the lines formed a beautiful posture. Lines flowed from the top to the bottom and then went to the details of the body, and a graceful figure came out in three minutes. The instructor who offered me a chance to sit in the class kept encouraging me to try to draw, but I politely refused.

Shortly after the croquis class, I came to think of trying to sketch the memory of my late mother in writing because there were some images of her as the precious past moments I'd like to keep in my mind. Looking back then I always shared a lot of things with my mother in every single way and my father also couldn't be excluded in some way. The best one in my mind is the purely innocent woman who was standing, leaning against a tree on the road. A woman in her forties was gleaming with her pinkish white complexion. Her forehead looked brighter with half covered curly hair. She put her hands behind the back and looked out over the crowd to find me. That look seemed very impressive to me as if she looked like a bashful Aphrodite.

Although she wasn't tall or gorgeous, she was a

good-looking woman in good shape with her long slender legs. As a teenage girl at that time, my mother looked the most beautiful woman in the world. Frankly speaking, I had never thought she was beautiful until that day. She had been just a mother who always kept home running and took care of family. Since we seldom ate out, I might have no chance to pay attention to what my mother looked like. One day she asked me on a date and we set the time for lunch when a mid-term exam in high school ended. The meeting place was at the bus station on Jong-ro near the popular restaurant. She arrived early and was waiting for me looking at the crowd, and I had found her first before she saw me. She wore an ivory colored blouse and a light pink skirt. Big double lid eyes with a sharp nose and full lips met my eyes.

For the first time in my life at age eighteen, I found out my mother was a beautiful woman. She often told me that her neighbors mistook her for an actor. That sounded ridiculous to me, thinking that she was a simple woman. But the image of her that day changed my view about my mother. She was a beautiful woman as well as a mother.

Since then, almost four decades had passed with many things like a college graduation, marriage and so on. And I almost forgot her face of that period even though I had spent time with her until she's gone. However, since she had been a part of my everyday life, backing me up anytime, she exists in my mind by fragments: her gesture, her smile, the light in her eyes, and her thick lips.

Especially I remember her broadened smile, along with my father's thoughtful smile shown to me whenever he talked to me despite he was a picky person. I feel how lucky I am since I had such a good parents who had been very devoted to me. Now I often sketch the contours of their smiles with good memories in the air that I breathe.

February 27, 2016

# Children's Day of 2016

The sun was shining through the bedroom window, but I was slow to open my sleepy eyes because I was up last night coughing almost until dawn. Today, the Children's Day, I was scheduled to visit a car dealership in Suwon, Kyunggi-do, to pick up a brand new car I bought a month ago. Although I was exhausted due to a lack of sleep, I sprang up from my bed and left home with my husband, anticipating something good as most children would do on a special day. Maybe I was thrilled about taking a long distance bus that I rarely had experienced since my college days. As my brother told me, I found the bus at the subway station entrance and the passengers were getting on the bus. After buckling up, we simultaneously closed eyes to make up for insufficient sleep. But soon uncomfortable seat bothered me, and I opened my eyes to try to enjoy the view through its window. The scenery wasn't special, rather it hurt my weary eyes. As I recognized each bus stop that I passed through, my expectation about exciting travel ended with disappointment. Besides we got off at a wrong bus stop, one more stop ahead of destination. Walking down the street under the hot sun to reach the next stop, I was putting my patience to the test.

The first part of my schedule seemed to be ruined, but on facing a polished white sedan I could feel myself recharged to go somewhere. Soon my brother who had lived nearby joined us and we were ready to hit the road in my new car taking his wife as well. The car rolled smoothly down the road heading to Kwangkyo, a district in Suwon. It was newly formed as a well-planned town a year ago and has grown to be the best neighborhood in Suwon. Speaking of Kwangkyo, I had visited it twice since last fall. On Korean Thanksgiving Day, one month after my mother passed away, my whole family got there to have dinner together. Back then I couldn't enjoy the place due to the loss of my loving mother--I just pretended to be happy with them not to ruin the holiday. And in March of this year I happened to pay attention to this new town when I visited Suwon again to attend my father's memorial service. After the memorial service, my sister-in-law suggested that we go to the lake Wonchun in Kwangkyo to walk around. At that moment I could remember that we were there last fall enjoying well-arranged high-rise buildings in an atmosphere of restfulness. And this third visit to Kwangkyo was somewhat exciting, expecting special cuisine at Avenue France, but long line of cars waiting for parking spaces made us turn around. We ended up having lunch in a restaurant nearby. Leaving the restaurant I thought the second part of my special day passed without any amusement.

Being slightly distorted I drove around the town area to find the designated streets for cafes as my sister-in-law guided.  On a dead end we found a cafe that looked the best.  I liked the interior of the shop decorated in European style and the smell of coffee.  Sitting down at an outdoor table, we were pleased with the spring breeze and beautiful flowers bloomed along the side of the stream.

The weather was perfect, coffee was excellent, brilliant sunbeams fell on the leaves, and we smelled the scent of spring in the air.  What a perfect day it was.  I didn't remember how long ago I enjoyed this fresh air beside this beautiful sidewalk with a stream. We lingered as long as we could over coffees and goodies.  At sunset we left for Lotte shopping mall near the Suwon station, the last course of the day. The scale of the mall was huge enough to be amazed at first, but soon too gigantic to adjust.  We gave up looking around the mall, trying to find a spot for rest. After light dinner I dropped my brother's couple and my husband and I were happy on the way back home with my brand new car.

At the parking garage of our apartment I was startled by the sound of a car horn when I shut the driver side door. Immediately I was afraid that I might get a defective car.

But I found that this happened because I locked the car door without turning off the ignition. It meant I got out of the car with the engine running. The sound of the engine was so quiet that I thought it was turned off. That was something funny to think about. It's been a long day today, but today would be a memorable day as Children's Day of a 59 year old woman.

May 5, 2016

# A Woman's Triumph

The sultry weather has kept up day by day ever since the middle of July. Exhausted and being aimless I crumpled in the couch and began to surf the internet looking for some volunteer work for the young as an English instructor. As looking over the headlines, my eyes were bent on a story that was about a sixteen year old handicapped student who got an admission into a university. Along with him, his mother was introduced as a strong-willed woman. It's not unlikely that a mother including me does her best for her child, especially on education because college background is meant to be a base to live a prosperous life. So a mother in Korea is supposed to spend money as much as she can. But this happens only to her biological child, not to an adopted child. Handicapped children are generally known to have a chance to be adopted by westerners, not by Korean families.

Much to my surprise, this woman decided to adopt a handicapped infant who had only one normal limb; his right arm had only two fingers and no legs. I was thrilled about the woman who had the guts and also curious about how she grew up before this adoption. Soon I found more information on the internet that she had a respectable father who always said that a day out of a week had to be spent for others to live like a decent human being. She had been led to some orphanages by her father since she was five, and she was accustomed herself to volunteer work. After a long time of volunteer work, one day in her late twenties she saw an infant with innocent smile and couldn't take her eyes off him. Soon she began the process of adopting, being encouraged by her daughter of her first marriage.

But she faced a barrier to adopt him in a short time because there had been a strict rule regarding adoption of handicapped orphans in order to prevent them from being abused as panhandlers. For six months she had tried to settle the matter without result, but she could hold the baby boy in her arm three days after her lengthy process of adoption was on TV in response to her request.

Since then her discipline for him has begun to make him live a happy life like an ordinary man. She indulged herself in raising her son no matter how hard the circumstances would be and she never gave up training him to be a normal boy. Although her adopted son and she together push themselves to overcome the particular situation, they realized the limitation in adapting to environments of regular schools. She couldn't help homeschooling him. Her son did everything as hard as he could to reach his adoptive mother's attempt. As time passed he found he would feel free and good when he was swimming. He practiced everyday manipulating his heavily handicapped body. At last when he was ready for higher education he took a school qualification exam and then passed, and finally was accepted to college as a sports major. In his successful life the boy's endless effort is praiseworthy, and behind him there has been a loving energizer, his caring adoptive mother along with his elder sister. The great strong-willed mother changed nobody to be a capable challenger to fulfill his dream.

August 16, 2016

# Miraculous Smile

Once or twice a week I toss and turn all night. Having too much coffee may cause insomnia, and sometimes I can't fall asleep without any reason. Almost every night I try hard to sleep by counting numbers and doing so-called 479 respiration method. As the clock's ticking my nerves are beginning to work, and then my mind begins to make a journey, thinking of what happened that day; the people I met, the place I went to, the things I hated, and so on. As the night goes on, the special memories come up in the darkness. Then I go back to the past, examine what I've done and I try to comfort myself hoping I did well. That has been absolutely okay as long as I bring myself to open my eyes when the sun rises.

By the way, since I made efforts to overcome my grief from losing my mother last year, the trivial things I used to recall in a sleepless night have turned into a series of my mother's days on a sickbed. Once I indulged in her days on a sickbed, I couldn't sleep thinking over and over what I was supposed to do to make her get well even though I knew nothing could be done. Being despaired I forced myself to recollect how much she felt proud of me and to remember her saying that she lived a happy life without any regret. Meanwhile something came to my mind so that I could feel relieved from my agony. That was a message that I was told in a Mass. A priest of the Catholic church preached that God would lead us to heaven in different ways. That message was a kind of relief recalling my mother's unbelievable smile. Up to then I had just remembered her weary face and a painful farewell to her that I couldn't bear. But I began to see the most painful scene of my mother's death as a splendid event.

On Monday, August 17, the phone rang and I heard that she was transferred to the ICU because she had lapsed into unconsciousness. I was in a hurry to see my mother who had been very weak two days ago. I was almost stunned and instantly became indignant with my second younger brother, a pastor, about delaying her baptism. I understood baptism would be a formal ceremony if belief in God was convincing, so she knew her faith would save her life as my brother told me. But my mother's conversion from Buddhism to Christianism had occurred two months before she passed away. It meant she wasn't yet religious seriously, though I pushed her to memorize the Lord's Prayer and advised her to take the Lord's hand if she got lost. My brother, at a loss, set the time for her baptism next day. I prayed to God all night for mercy that the Lord gave her time to be baptized. The next morning she looked a bit better even though she couldn't blink her eyes at all, let alone paralyzed. Foolishly enough I thought she would live like that for more months when I saw her in bed. I leaned close to her and whispered she should stay awaken to be baptized at 5 p.m. and hold Jesus's hand. She had been lying on her side like a stone until the baptism began to perform. Around her my first brother, a pastor brother and his wife, my third sister-in-law and I were standing with hands put together.

The performing pastor began to talk about Jesus who came to save us and the heaven that we all aspire to enter someday, stroking gently her shoulder. His voice sounded so clear enough to catch every word about the Lord. All of sudden my mother moved both tips of her lips upward and made a big smile with a pleased look. All of us were amazed with that miraculous smile. In fact she was paralyzed and she couldn't even shed a tear when I was shaking her with desperation a few minutes before the baptism. But she smiled as if she welcomed Jesus who might hold her hand and walk along to Heaven. Her smile must be shown in acknowledgement of the Lord's kindness. She might be joyful enough to move her paralyzed lips. That moment was the notion to us that Heaven is for real. I recited "Glory be to the Father, and to the Son and to the Holy Spirit, As it was in the beginning, is now, and will be forever. Amen"

What a glorious moment it was! We all said 'Amen' with amazing grace and she went back to the motionless condition, but looked very peaceful. For the past nine months I hadn't remembered her smile because I was so painful. I was tormented by a feeling of guilt; I blamed myself for her illness. I was sorry that she hadn't been a Christian until I asked her to accept Jesus Christ as the Lord two months before she died. But thankfully, she was baptized at the last minutes of her life. In a word, God led my mother to heaven in a different way. I thank God for everything as always. Through my mother's miraculous smile I become feel at ease about my loss and believe that Heaven is for real.

August 28, 2016

# Chocolate

In a rainy afternoon I could feel relief from suffocating heat which lasted all summer long. While looking out the window and breathing in fresh air, I was in the mood to enjoy this lazy afternoon. With a cup of coffee and some chocolate goodies I sat in front of TV. A little while after flipping channels, I saw an actress who looked familiar to me and my flipping stopped on that channel. It was the movie 'Chocolat(2000).' Long time ago I would see it, but it caught my eyes again because it seemed like a movie 'An Education' which gave an idea to viewers what the real education was like along with warm and touching mood. I was also impressed with actors' excellent performances.

Expecting another good impression I watched 'Chocolat' focusing on each scene, each facial expression and conversations. The first scene I started to see was a woman, Vianne, in a colorful dress making chocolate goodies in a shop. She just moved in a French village and wanted to stay awhile by running a chocolaterie 'Maya'. As a young mother as well as an expert chocolatier she had lived different places with her daughter. When she was almost ready to open, she was visited by a village mayor who was known stubborn as well as abstinence. He warned her not to open the chocolate shop because the forty days of Lent began and the villagers had to observe the days.

Since townspeople followed him whatever he said, they were afraid of getting into the shop. In the meantime as an atheist she ignored the mayor and kept making sweet things with amusement. Townspeople seemed to be excited, but concealed their lust for sweet chocolates in fear of the mayor. Nobody challenged his command, even the priest had to follow whatever the mayor instructed. While most villagers evaded the shop, an elderly landlady showed up first without caring about what would happen. After being treated with a cup of cocoa cordially by Vianne, the landlady became a main customer and then a woman who suffered from her abusive husband. Both women fell under the spell of Vianne, so to speak. A little later the landlady's grandson joined. All of them were served chocolate stuff after being tricked by Vianne's mind reading and began to support Vianne to find a way out from their agonies for themselves.

When the mayor's objection of her grew more and more because of Vianne's audacious access to townspeople, the band of gypsies anchored off the coast of the village to camp. Soon after unloading their stuff, the leader of the gypsies fell in love with Vianne after tasting 'Maya's goodies under her spell. Several days later the birthday party thrown for the landlady by Vianne became the culmination to let townspeople's abstinent manners go away. Only the mayor remained as her enemy against her nice spell. In consequences there came a crisis that Vianne would come close to packing to leave after she knew the mayor set fire to the boat of gypsies and let her lover leave the town. But she gave up because she saw the people's earnest desire to be together with her.

The day before Easter Sunday the mayor decided to break into the shop to mess up, but as facing sweet things he surrendered himself to his nature by eating chocolates which had been displayed in the showcase for Easter Sunday. On Easter Sunday the mayor, totally changed, showed up thanking Vianne for forgiving his shameful act, and everybody in the village celebrated Easter. They were ready to resume their lives in peace and love. The townspeople who had been bystanders with scorn accepted Vianne, a total stranger one time, as a neighbor with warm hospitality. As Vianne noticed that the north wind grew weary, her gypsy man came back to live with her and her daughter. The movie ended suggesting their wandering life would settle down soon.

After movie, I could feel myself getting choked up for a while; thinking love and gratitude. Although the townspeople, in a time of self-denial and abstinence, couldn't show their true feelings, they had been in need of sharing the joys and sorrows of life. Vianne timely showed up and made them change with the power of chocolate. Sweetness truly may be the best remedy for change melting their oppressed hearts. Sweet things seem to have power to conquer one's mentality. When people are stressed out and feel gloomy, they mostly seem to find medications or alcohol drinks. But real solution may underlie in the sweet stuff. Chocolate, the most favorite goody in the world, may let people feel relaxed and happy to find new joyful lives, and yet obesity can't be excluded as well. It must be hard to wrestle with temptation towards overeating. Getting a piece of sweet chocolate will be an attempt to test the will, let alone happiness. But there will be no problem as long as people don't care about their figures. That's why people may love chocolate regardless of age. Funnily enough, I've considered to be a chocolatier as my future job for a short time after the movie.

September 7, 2016

# Precious Moments in Buenos Aires

A long time ago, in 1981 I flew to Buenos Aires with my husband who had been scheduled to work for the Korean embassy to Argentina for three years. As a newlywed bride, being married after dating for only two months, getting started in South America was a big challenge since I had never been in the western world at the time, let alone a language barrier. And Argentina would be the last place to live in my head because of a vast distance. As expected, the first scene I saw on arrival was the same as I had seen in the popular travelogue. People were unfamiliar to me unlike those in New York where we went through by staying two nights before Buenos Aires. I had a hunch it would take time to get used to the smell in the air that couldn't be expressible. Besides, I was homesick for Seoul missing my parents and people close to me so much. After about two weeks or so passed, one thing went through my head: a Spanish grammar book to learn on my own. Now that I was supposed to stay for a period of time, I had no choice but adapting myself to the city. Best of all, I had to speak Spanish to make a conversation with the gynecologist before our honeymoon baby was due. As I focused on studying, I could make progress on speaking Spanish only, not reading. Communicating with locals gave me some vitality to explore my neighborhood. I began to get over homesickness and then make several friends who came from the US and Europe. There's a person who I still want to hear from. She is Rossana Pronesti, an American college student at the time who visited her parents. After we met in an American Womens Club, we were close watching movie together and visiting each other's place since her parents' house was a block away. I was busy day and night meeting friends and eating out with my husband. My growing baby bump couldn't obstruct me from going out, even though my husband worried about my safety from day to day. Things were not going bad as he thought and the city seemed safe to go around to some degree. Thinking back then I had no fear in doing what I wanted to and wasn't afraid of local people.

There was an episode with taxi driver while I used to visit my gynecologist for a regular checkup. One day, on my way home I took a taxi alone as usual, and I was startled with the taxi fare that costed fifty thousand pesos, ten times than usual fares. That situation left me at a loss. Soon I remained calm and opened the passenger door shouting "llama policia"-call the police. And then the taxi driver, astonished, said "five thousand pesos" and I got off. He might think a young pregnant oriental woman, who was told a seventeen year old girl by the locals, would be scared to give the taxi fare as much as he wanted, but he was wrong. Except this happening everything seemed great: a certain street for only passersby, shops, streets filled with movie theaters and local people. One of the interesting places was an Argentine traditional market which was across our apartment.

One day being asked by a woman whose husband also worked for the Korean embassy, I went to the market. The huge container shaped market had compartments for stores which sold different kinds of grocery. Each store displayed its special stuff that I didn't know because I had never cooked before. Unfortunately I couldn't finish shopping that day because of morning sickness I had once for all, and that visit was the first and the last. After that outing I stepped out into my neighborhood alone everyday touring around shops and restaurants, and tried to memorize street names that I passed through. Several months later I became audacious enough to take a bus to know the city further, even though I wasn't fluent in

Spanish. Before leaving home, I studied the map how I would reach the places I designated. I still remember the streets that looked lovely as well as polished and good looking people. The locals, relatively small, were so friendly that I couldn't feel I was in a foreign country. In the meantime I was also busy to find a good doctor for me and a new apartment for three of us because I couldn't like the place where we had moved in as soon as we arrived. In December when I felt relaxed adapting myself to the city, I gave birth to my only son, DaeWon. He was a 'porteno' in Spanish because he was born in Buenos Aires. He was tall and heavy and grew so fast that his pediatrician always asked me whether his father was tall whenever I visited.

A few months after his birth the Falkland War broke out between March and June 1982 as a conflict between Argentina and the United Kingdom over the Falkland Islands. The consequences came along with the low value of pesos and I could hire a full time nanny of German origin for my son. Luckily enough, she took care of my son with love and made every meal for us as well. I had a lot of free time from the morning enough to meet local friends all day long. For two years we lived in the best district of the city. That fashionable neighborhood where my son started his life was near the central part of the city.

I could see stylish women and cultured men there more often than in other parts of the city. I recall those days were the best time in my life because I was young, energetic and well equipped to do everything I wanted to. I flourished in Buenos Aires. As I recall these unforgettable times, there comes precious memories along with my only son, DaeWon. Like other babies he wanted to stick with me from dawn till night. But I usually read books when I was home and then went out almost every day. He might think his mother was not good for him, and yet he never was impatient with me. One day he took a pen to scribble on the page while I was reading, and was blocked by me. He stopped doing it as soon as I told and never did it again in front of me. Several days later when I opened the book that I had read to continue to read, I was astonished at a mass of scribbles done on many pages. DaeWon behaved himself; he scribbled while I was away. The second event he showed months later was more shocking. One morning I was watching TV in a bed and my son came in whining. So I told him he was not supposed to be whiny because I hated it. He glanced at my face and ran away to his room next to mine. And I heard a big cry for a few minutes and then I saw his shadow on the wall through the half-open door standing to calm down. After a few second he lightly pushed the door and said 'mommy' with a big smile on his face to please me. He behaved himself even though I didn't teach him. Now, thirty two years later, I still cherish precious moments of those days in Buenos Aires.

September 17, 2016

# Memories of Living in America

Almost eleven years have passed since my family moved in the current place. That's the longest time we've ever stayed in one home. Until then we've moved at intervals of two or three years. There were several reasons: too big for three of us, too far from my husband's workplace and the university I went to, to live close to our friend, or because of my husband's transfer from Chicago to Seoul. Looking back then there was one thing in common; I was tireless and enjoyed the tension I could feel in an unfamiliar circumstance. But now after I settled in our current home I no longer pack for moving. Instead, as time goes on, I feel nostalgia for the old days, and especially recall the past memories of living in the United States every now and then. We had lived seven apartments in the United States for nine years, all rented. Moving from one place to another in a foreign country was a challenging process. Even though I got accustomed to move since Buenos Aires where I lived in three different places for three years, the whole thing about moving wasn't as simple as ABC. The first place we moved in was University Village located in Athens, a university town in Georgia.

As my husband had started his graduate school there four months before I joined him with DaeWon, our three year old son, he couldn't help finding a place for us instead of me. After being advised and led by a Korean student, Mr.Paik who became a long-time friend, he unpacked his baggage next to the Paik's place. The three story building in which most residents rented were students of UGA seemed to be about three decades old. The building was quite old enough I could smell for mold when we entered the hallway. On the first day, while we were dragging our large bags to reach the third floor by taking the stairs, we had to be escorted by a pack of cats that suddenly appeared out of nowhere around the building. They were walking together with us shooting coquettish glances to make eye contact with us. At the door the cats stopped altogether waiting to be invited. I was nervous with them for fear of their stepping inside. We swiftly walked in the porch and shut the door behind them and relieved. It was a very long day from Seoul via Chicago to Atlanta airport and finally stood in the apartment to settle down in a small town where wild cats were roaming in the street. Being welcomed by my husband only, my challenge to living abroad like in Buenos Aires began. Since my husband had never decided where to live or what to buy, I just let him go to work and did the rest on my own. A little while after being relieved, I could look around inside: two bedrooms, a bathroom, a small kitchen and a living room. As the first dwelling place we would stay while waiting for a vacant apartment in the family housing of the university, this old apartment complex wasn't too bad to endure except cats and mice. The cats I saw on the first day were catchers, in a manner of speaking. It seemed likely that cats were supposed to hang around to catch mice that frequently were everywhere in sight, even in the lower cabinet of the kitchen. Even though I made a fuss over the trace that a mouse left, such as a rat hole and a torn plastic bag of rice, and called the janitor to check the kitchen asking him to do something to stop them, I soon got used to living with them that way. My son, DaeWon, who had been with his nanny or my mother until then, seemed to be satisfied with the new environment. In spite of being with me all day long before he attended a preschool, he never looked tiresome. Rather, he was content with things around him and tried to do his best whatever he was doing to be a quick learner.

Luckily, three months later we had a phone call from the university that we could move to a family housing, the complex that was built for foreign students in the outskirts of the campus. It took ten minutes by a shuttle bus from the campus to a family housing and there came a school bus for children. As I loved my neighbors and the rural scenery, gradually the small town began to grow on me. I made friends with the locals and people from around the world, including Koreans. Especially DaeWon was lucky enough to meet his homeroom teacher in the kindergarten. It was so sweet of her that everybody cared for her. She always smiled when her eyes met anybody's. Her smile sweetened the class and encouraged my son to be positive and active as well. When I finished my third quarter in graduate school, we had to move to Atlanta, Georgia because my husband began to practice law at a law firm.

In Atlanta we could afford to rent a better apartment in a quiet decent neighborhood. DaeWon started his first grade and I transferred to Georgia State University to continue for a master's degree in art history. He adjusted to a new school environment easily and I met

Ludmila, a Polish woman, in a meeting which was held for business women working in Atlanta. I got along with her having lunch together at her apartment because she was a good cook; I loved her special dishes like lasagne. Atlanta, known as the setting of the movie 'Gone With The Wind', wasn't impressive to me. I just practiced driving by taking a highway to reach Georgia State University in downtown. Since then I could overcome my fear of entering the tollway and I became a fast driver as I tried to reduce commuting time, and I handled driving entirely as a family driver.

In summer 1990, we moved in a townhome in the suburbs of Chicago, Illinois. Soon after we settled down in that townhouse, I realized my decision on that area was wrong for me and my husband. It was too far to commute on a daily basis; it took almost one hour to get Chicago downtown. The best thing I could remember in that place was Teresa, my good neighbor, who was an immigrant from Poland where she worked as a journalist but then in Chicago as a full time waitress. As she worked in the evening, we had been together chatting in the daytime once in a while and she used to babysit DaeWon for free. After experiencing heavy snow in Wheeling, we moved to Glenview where we could save time to get downtown.

Since most of residents in Glenview were Jewish people who mostly had a deep interest in education, I could feel at ease about the school my son would go to. To tell the truth I felt sorry for DaeWon since we moved so often that he couldn't have intimate friends. Thankfully, he had positive attitude to what he faced and didn't cause any trouble in school, saying he went to school for learning. When my son attended Lyon Elementary School, I still remember a boy, John, who bullied my son. As I warned his mother that I could file the suit about what he had done and then regularly showed up in his class working as a volunteer, my son regained the impaired reputation.

In 1993 when we went back to Chicago from Seoul where we had lived for two years due to my husband's work, I had to get readmission to continue my graduate studies at UIC and my son also transferred to Maple Junior High School. At this time in Chicago I could be familiar with the suburbs and narrow down the area to find a condominium located next to a junior high school for my son. We should find a place within walking distance of his school because I would be away too far in the daytime to pick him up at school. We were all content as long as my son could be safe walking home even though I had to take my husband to railroad station to let him commute to work before I drove to my school by car almost four days a week. The apartment we moved in was in the Northbrook County. In this district I could see more Jewish families than in Glenview. That meant I could meet ardent parents and teachers in DaeWon's junior high school and neighbors who would stick to the rules of the condominium complex; for example, when the kid bounced the basket ball in the hallway, a neighbor who peeped and heard that noise reported right away to the management office to fine the kid 100 dollars for breaking the rules. We loved to live in this neighborhood because we were law-abiding people. DaeWon did well in school, getting excellent grades and winning math competition held in the state of Illinois. He seemed enjoy his life in Northbrook, but I could feel he missed Korean school life that he had experienced for more than one year. And he often said he would like to get into a university in Korea, especially SNU, the nation's top university. That sounded ridiculous at first because he had only one and a half year education in Korea.

But I decided to give him a chance to turn his dream into reality for a trial of period. As long as he wanted it, there was no reason to think twice and I set the time to leave Chicago to enroll DaeWon at a junior high school in Seoul. As soon as I earned a master's degree, I put my idea into action. Before we left for Seoul, my job was to search for a place for my husband who would stay alone apart from us because he still had to work. Since he worked downtown, I found one near Lake Michigan on Lakeshore Drive and signed a monthly lease for a studio apartment. Needless to say, my husband was content with it. When I was ready for a new start, two things came to mind. I was thinking that my ridiculous decision would be absurd in shaping my son's future even though he had wanted it. Since he did well in school so that he could go to a good college and get a good job in America, going to Seoul to live his life was an adventure. In my case, living in Chicago was also a better choice because I changed my major to graphic design to work as a designer in Chicago by running a studio. But I gave up a wish that I had for the sake of my son and we flew to Seoul at last.

Looking back, for two years and a half in Chicago, the last period in the United States, we had lived well enough to keep good memories. Living in America for nine years as a whole was good experience for DaeWon; he learned how to survive this world by adapting himself to five different schools. Ultimately he made it, in other words, he entered SNU. At some point in our lives we would ask whether we were on the right track. I believe I made a right decision for my son who began adjusting to life in Seoul as a ninth grade student and got a good job enjoying social networking. After 20 years, I still remember everything I've experienced in America such as universities I went to, apartments I lived, roads I went through and people I met in school and in my neighborhoods.

September 21, 2016

# Truth

I couldn't take my eyes off the TV screen while I was watching the movie 'A Good Marriage(2014)'. I was extremely curious about how Darcy, who found the formidable secret of her husband, an accountant, would deal with such a unsolvable circumstance. After a 25 happy marriage, not only her heart was broken but also she faced two things that couldn't be handled in a normal way. Her adult children--a daughter, bride to be and a son--had to be spared from their father's criminal career as a serial killer and she also had to survive from her husband who was meticulous enough to check and control her everyday life. Known as a warm-hearted father to her children, her husband was a perfect family man who always cared for her by doing household chores and sharing his hobby--collecting coins-- although he seemed to lust for other women. But when Darsy happened to find several ID cards of women, who had been on air as victims of serial murders, from a small box hidden in a garage while her husband was out of town for work, she realized her good marriage definitely would end. Besides, she found out that the earrings, a gift of 25th anniversary, given by her sweet husband were those of a victim's, one of twelve raped and murdered women. She became furious and terrified of her husband's cruelty. All of sudden she seemed to feel standing in the middle of nowhere.

Meanwhile her husband who planned to do another murder that night turned back home as soon as he felt a tremble in her voice over the phone. And in their bedroom she was told his explanation of bad deeds along with an implicit threat, and she shivered after all. From then on she was cautious about whatever she did. She behaved the same as usual to avoid her husband's doubt which would be her attempt to report to the police. It seemed likely that she lived like stepping on a thin coat of ice. In such circumstance, she seemed to focus on protecting her children from the reality that might be revealed nationwide soon. After her daughter's wedding she was watching for an opportunity to get rid of him.

One afternoon her husband became highly elated over the priceless coin he found in a piggy-bank. As she created some mood cheering him up on finding a valuable coin, her husband, being deceived by the way she used to be, offered her to have dinner at a fine restaurant in trying to get their relationship back on track. After getting back home, the canny serial killer fooled by her seduction climbed upstairs with their usual sodas floating on air, and then he was pushed hard to fall downstairs by her. A few minutes later she gagged him desperately with all her strength because he seemed to gain consciousness from concussion. Finally she found him dead and called to get help. She solved the problem; she saved both her children and herself. She wasn't clumsy as her husband pointed out all the time but scrupulous. Several days after his funeral, she was visited by an old retired detective who secretly had investigated the serial murder by himself. Since he knew by intuition that she had committed perfect crime, he seemed to try to disclose a crime which had been disguised as an accident. But in the end he let her go saying she had done the right thing.

After this movie the matter of truth comes to mind; cover up the truth or uncover the truth. This problem would bring a dichotomy of view. It seems hard to say whether the truth has to be revealed. Speaking of justice, the criminal should be open to the public and pay the price for criminal act. That's the way most people think. But for innocent offspring of the criminal who are supposed to be exposed to the public that means their lives cannot be like the way it used to be. They seem like a sacrifice against their will. The truth everybody wants to know becomes an invisible weapon to make another victim.

Watching both Darcy, a leading role in the movie, who covered up the truth of the serial murders and an old detective who turned a blind eye to her intentional killing of her husband, I could feel quite relieved. Sometimes the truth that has to be buried forever may be a beautiful thing.

September 29, 2016

# Marriage

In my college days, marriage was meant to be a required course for a life of happiness. As young people were aged 20 something, they expected to meet someone to make a family. They were taking it for granted that they should marry before it's too late. Once a woman got married, she usually gave up her career and devoted her life to her kids and cooking. And a man also sacrificed himself to be a family man. And we called it a good life. In the 1980s people's everyday life was simple. People just worked hard to reach the goal they set for better life without distracting themselves. They couldn't waste time to do things for themselves.

But at the same time, in the midst of hectic life, most of them were willing to spend some time to help other people. Living as human beings was supposed to be meaningful in the spirit of sharing.

To this day most people of my age think their offspring should marry after they have jobs to follow our ways of life. But as things change, many of young people of today like to stay single. My only son also has the same idea about marriage; He seems to be entitled to live his life as free as a bird. Today people seem to focus on their own things and their cell phones as they are spreading widely around the world. People of young ages chase meaningless things through cell phones and they can't go through a day without them. As the function of cell phone becomes enhanced year by year, especially young people's perspective on life looks like changing. They are inclined to avoid responsibility for the members of family and like to pursue pleasure in their own space.

In terms of relationship, they seem to need just

partners, not wives nor children. What the younger generation chases seems to be a free life and fun. As I try to conform to their contemporary life style, I begin to think of them on their sides because there has been the gap between generations. And then a while ago there was an event that made me reconsider whether marriage would be necessary to life. One day my close friend told me about her psychological pressure caused by her husband. When I heard her who had been abused mentally throughout her marriage up to now, my heart was broken. Up to then I thought she had been cared all the time by her husband, but she had been suffered under her husband's self centered personality.

She already had gone through some rocky times for the past few years and then she's just getting started to overcome. She should have been awarded by her husband. But on the contrary, her husband blamed her for what happened to them and she was told that everything she had done was wrong. I was frightened by his mental abuse toward her, and yet I had nothing to do for her. The only thing I could say that I would pray for her though one of her close friends suggested to separate with him for the time being. In this situation, she seemed to be caught in dilemma considering her current state as the heart in her family supporting her children despite her spouse's disregard; she can't give up her marriage this way.

If I had been in her shoes, I would have been in the same dilemma. And I told my friend calmly that she'd better put up with her problems to keep her home safe, reminding her of his merits because I doubted she could deal with a broken marriage which would mean a failure in life to her. We, in our late fifties, were supposed to be part of our in-laws no matter what the marriage conditioned. That sounds absolutely ridiculous these days, but most middle aged married women have tried to keep their lives normal at the sacrifice of themselves. And then I also informed her that I began to treat my husband with compassion after I was baptized into the Catholic church and as a companion for life who can share. To my delight, she seemed to draw strength from me and said she could deal with the problem by giving love to him.

Every now and then, I have a chance to hear about a home problem since many of Korean married women like to boast or backbite their spouses while they chat over the trifles of life. For the most of time I become the listener telling them what I would do if I were in their situations. And I realize that every situation people face in their marriage must not be easy due to a difference in personality and attitude. At any moment a couple can collide insisting on each one's thought and then there comes an obvious sign of discord. At last love becomes an empty shell as they proceed with the marriage. The man ascribes his failure to his spouse and vice versa. At this point the disadvantage of marriage may have fallen on women if women had no financial power since they gave up their professional career. A woman who believed in her husband's love feel betrayed without job to survive the outside world.

Perhaps I might go a little too far with the bad case of marriage because this doesn't need to be related with the younger generation. As of now, the young generation doesn't care about marriage itself. Even if they get married, they are contemplating divorce when they find some disagreement and see some friends around break up with their spouses. Besides, they don't want to put themselves under some restraint and dislike being interfered with their comfort, let alone their privacy. They have been even encouraged to stay single by their mothers unless they met qualified ones. Mothers of my age around sometimes think unqualified son-in-laws are useless for their daughters.

Under these tricky circumstances, any adults including me can't persist in saying that marriage is a blessing. Nonetheless, as a woman who keeps marriage stable, I'd like to let young people know that being together with children makes life easier in the long run. This may sound boring to young people who never imagine how their future life would be. But they should question whether the dramatic world in the cell phone they are dreaming every minute of everyday could provide them with a meaningful life with the warmth of humanity in some way. And parents who don't care that their offspring live as singles should ask themselves whether they are doing right.

In some respects my view on marriage may be absurd since a matter of marriage must be personal and nobody can be sure that marriage is going to be successful as long as one lives. But I'd like to express my personal two points about marriage. First, both personal and legal bond make a life stable and affluent. This point can be understood in old age. Second, I assume both success and failure in marriage boil down to one thing: thoughtfulness. I mean the odds of success in marriage may depend on how they treat each other; if a spouse behaves on the side of the other, there won't be any psychological wound left. Mutual understanding makes the relationship between husband and wife turn into a true friendship. The clock is ticking away and

the growing number of wrinkles reflected in the mirror
seems to tell us something.

October 20, 2016

 Green

The color I like most is green. Just looking at the color green makes me happy. I love watching all kind of green stuff everywhere around me: at home, in the street, in the shopping center, on the mountain and so on. So almost every weekend from early spring to late fall I go to the mountain with my husband to see green things. In early spring yellowish green trees seem to greet me and then I feel like a young girl again. As I breathe fresh air and move upward step by step, I feel my body absorbing energy from the forest. In summer I love to rest in the middle of hiking to enjoy dark green leaves of the forest. Hiking is not my cup of tea but collateral for appreciation of the green hue of leaves. In fall I just watch fallen leaves, waiting for spring.

Several months ago my fondness of the color green extended to such a field as the TV series "I'm a nature man" that I happened to watch by chance. At first the program didn't catch my eyes because each man in the TV series was shabbily dressed living in a natural wilderness. They looked like bummers who have no place to stay or family. But, since I was in grief over the loss of my mother at the time, I didn't care about their appearance. I just saw green in the background and began to keep my eye on it. And by watching one by one, I found that each mountain man came in the woods with despair. Mostly they had been either deadly sick diagnosed with fatal diseases such as terminal cancer or failed in their entire lives by being defrauded of their properties.

They started their new lives as if frontiers did in the new world. They didn't care wild animals like boars while staying in tents or under the fallen leaves every night before they built their humble huts. Mostly they should have abandoned everything including their families to get over the trauma. Working as hard as possible implied rebuilding their lives and they could get themselves back on their feet. They just wanted to live by provision of nature. Since they were desperate to survive from their misfortune, they couldn't help leaving the world they once had belonged to and chose the woods. The environment surrounded them diffused energy and gave hope to outlive their adversities.

After they stepped in the woods where there was no electricity, they felt the mountain embrace their lives and give another chance. They began to regain their confidence and could believe their lives would be healed by nature. The mountain filled with green leaves provided the best cure for all sickness to those who were so hurt by people or suffered by hard lives that they couldn't recuperate in the city. I saw them work from dawn till dusk gardening nearby ground, growing vegetables, raising livestock, and climbing mountain to dig into herbs or mushrooms for themselves. In a few years they pulled themselves out of their hardships and began to indulge in their second life in the deep woods. They just entrusted themselves to the nature with respect and followed it leaving behind modern civilization.

People around me wonder how I love to watch this kind of program that seems to be for the elderly or middle aged men. Strangely enough, I can feel at ease while I watch woods, bushes, gardens and listen to their struggles for survival along with their earnest efforts. As they stroll up the mountain to find some fresh edible herbs as alternative medicine and work in their own farm to feed themselves, my eyes follow them watching green in trees and crops. And then I realize they are chosen to be happy even though they couldn't have any choice but the mountain to get out of their bad luck. I found the common thing in them was their diligence with meticulous attention to detail.

After I mastered this TV series of the past years

and still watch it once a week, I could feel better and better. The color green proved its powerful energy to heal people. Tracing this green color makes me cast my eyes over human drama based on real-life stories these days. In the story I could see green trees and bushes in the background with excitement and feel good with a touching story. Now as winter is around the corner, green things in the forest turn red and yellow and I'm waiting for spring to come soon.

October 25, 2016

# At My Age

When I found a phrase like 'the old age' in the essay I was reading, I skipped it and went on to another piece because I didn't want to know about that life. I thought I wasn't meant to grow old. To this day I have a good memory that makes me do whatever I want to do and still I work out regularly to keep my body in shape to look healthy. And of course, I've also kept in mind that I shouldn't push myself to excess. Since I'm independent-minded, I've thought that I wouldn't let my only son look out for me in case of my sickness. Though it's too early to say for certain, I keep in mind that by the time I depend on someone's care, my life wouldn't be worth living. This sounds sad, but no one can evade the reality of old age. Needless to say, this is 20 years away at least. This thoughtful love for my son helps me do something for myself. So, I exercise as often as I can, have a good meal, lower my speed and try to do my best not to look my age. There was a small event that makes me smile. One day I was in the elevator with a young mother, a neighbor, and her daughter and by the time I was getting off, she told her daughter to step aside to let a "big sister" through. I was amused a lot to be called a "big sister."

But things have changed as I'm beginning to feel weary these days. Unlike last year, I become discouraged a bit and try to accept that the age thing is unavoidable. Although I never imagined how I would become old and I thought the world of old people wouldn't exist for me, now I understand old age is a fact of life and I'm entering old age with the same feeling as other middle-aged people may have. Shortly after I turned 59, I became aware that my point of view on things around me has changed. Speaking of people's looks, these days almost everyone passing by me seems young to me. Not long ago I thought people would be older than me when I ran into them in the elevator where I had no choice but to look furtively, but surprisingly, I recently see most people look a lot younger than me. To my eye, even a woman in her mid forties seems like a twenty something. Except grey-haired people, every person looks young to me, and this makes me feel strange. Maybe it would be relative to my age. Though I try not to feel conscious of my age when I look myself in the mirror, I can't stop my mind from working in different ways.

Thirty five years ago marrying a man who met conditions that my father wished right after graduation from college was a starting point in my adult life. A new life with my unfamiliar husband began abroad. Since I had no proper chance to work in the competitive professional world, I had to find what I could do as an alternative work to compensate for it in a foreign country. I was good at speaking Spanish as a result of hard practice on my own and took part in some group activity in the city I lived. When I lived in the US, I went to three different graduate schools because of frequent moving. What I still regret to this day was my quick decision to give up changing my major to mechanical engineering. Because I had to take undergraduate classes for three years before graduate study, I stopped trying to get involved in the world of engineering. Looking back then I was in my mid thirties at the time and I could finish it at age 40. I was young then compared to what I'm doing now. I even took a exam for a certain license at the age of 53 and started to learn another foreign language recently.

For twelve years abroad I did my best raising my son and finishing graduate school as well. Until last year, I had worked in different fields, helping my son to enter college and I've been tied up and spent my everyday life busy living enthusiastically not to disappoint myself. I only saw forward taking care of things that were lying in front of me and never looked back. I enjoyed my life without complaining and just doing something within my means.

These days as I feel my age, I begin to think about what would be good to do at my age. I don't try to find work though I have a short blank in my history. As I can get by on the minimum due to my spirit of non-possession, I just enjoy having the time of my life and feeling grateful for everyday life. Most of my friends at my age spend their time on a tight schedule doing things they like or have to. I didn't see any middle aged women spend their time in idleness. They seem to burn off their energy as if they can't let their time pass by in vain. When compared with them, I have a low stamina and I just enjoy being at home where no one bothers me. In my free time, sometimes I bring up the question of how I should live at my age. There's no answer to that and no one can advise what to do. Those who are at my age stand on their own feet without any advisor to guide them. In a sense, people at my age face the reality of exploring the new world of old age.

As I'm about to reach at this stage, I feel that my past days seem nothing but a dream when I look back upon them and I realize life rarely goes as planned. As of now, I try to spend my time mostly at home on trivial things, considering my physical ability. This sounds a bit miserable, but luckily for me I have positive emotions by reminding myself that good things happen to good people. This helps me change my attitude to see people and things. Unlike old days I try to see things and people positively whatever one may do. I also find that my happiness comes from the happiness of others. A song, 'you were born to be loved.... ,'gives me a small smile.

Whatever my sense tells me to feel, I should behave in accordance with my age and keep in mind that all matters depend on the state of mind. Sometime later I'm going to search for what I should do based on my physical condition. And now I'm saying to myself, it's time to make myself available for the second half of life.

November 1, 2016

# The Wrong Direction

By the time I saw leaves in the street turn red and yellow, I thought I should go for an outing to enjoy the scene of fall. It wasn't until last Sunday afternoon in late November that I made up my mind to go out with my husband for a breath of fresh air. In that morning I got up early unusually and looked out the window to check the weather, and then woke up my husband making a fuss to be ready to leave home as early as possible. My husband seemed to be surprised because he used to see me stay idling at home watching outdoor scenery on TV every weekend. I told him that I would drive him to the park where I found on the internet.

As my husband, Yoong, had been my follower, he just hopped in the car and tuned in-car navigation system to set the destination.

In the passenger seat he stared at the screen of navigation device to check the route that we would be going down. We hit the road to the park-- Inchon Grand Park--located close to the city of Shiheung. As a family driver, I already searched for the destination and figured out how to get there and return home. I drove the car through the highways that I planned to take. Even though it didn't rain when we departed from home, the rain was still holding off. We were talking in the car how nice we were out of home, let alone autumn leaves. While the navigation device enunciated directions in a woman's voice, I assured myself of the right way. Some neighborhoods we passed by looked newly formed with high rise buildings. We were amazed how fast the barren land turned into a well developed town.

After following two road signs of the park entrance, we arrived at the paid parking lot nicely and walked into the roofed flat column entrance. The tree lined path welcomed us although trees weren't as beautiful as those in photos online because yellow and red leaves were dry and withered. We looked round and found the outdoor museum in which huge natural stones were placed. Each oddly shaped piece of stone was overwhelming along with its huge size. Strolling between stones was an unusual amusement. We continued walking in silence looking around and found a glass edifice with a sign saying "Botanical Garden." I was amazed with so many different kinds of cactuses inside the garden. After the long walk we found a cafeteria that meant to satisfy us with the joy of eating. We were much happier with edible things as the proverb says, "A loaf of bread is better than the song of many birds." We chatted about the park that would be a favorable place to visit again. With full of satisfaction, I started the engine and my husband tuned the navigation system. I already planned how I would reach home, but the navigation told us to take the opposite way. At that moment I followed its guide with doubt. I was sure that the direction I heard was wrong, but my husband suggested me to follow it. As soon as I made a right turn instead of left, I realized that I took the wrong way because that direction would take us home twice as late as expected. There was no U-turn lane and I couldn't help keep going.

At that moment I was beside myself with my stupidity and jerked out an insult at the navigation device. And then I left the highway at the next exit ignoring the voice and proceeded by following my instinct on the direction. I didn't care about a loud car horn blast behind us when I tried to find the possible route for the highway to take the right way. After wandering the streets I got on the highway, and soon the silence fell in the car. I also said nothing feeling ashamed of my short temper. For a while I had no idea how I could make him feel comfortable with me. In a calm voice I began to talk about what the park was like, and it helped change the mood in the car.

Thinking back then I should have held my temper and behave myself with patience because it was no big deal although we would be lost on some unfamiliar street.

But, speaking of my state of mind, I was so mad at the guiding voice and my husband's suggestion that I couldn't help showing my discontent by driving the car carelessly. In fact, going in the opposite direction was not that bad enough to get mad like a hornet. If I thought positively, that could be the chance to get to know the city for some other time. But my mind went blank for a moment and I started blaming my husband in mind for a wrong decision. All faults were ridiculously attributed to him. And I didn't hide what I was thinking and said 'you sloppy bitch' to the device. My husband must have been uneasy about the whole situation. He might realize that he was demeaned by me, but thankfully, he seemed to take it lightly since he knew me short tempered and there was no offense intended.

That evening at home I repented of my foolish

conduct. I thought that my typical trait--losing my temper easily-- had improved since I began to manage to hold back my anger after being baptized. But there was still a long way to go before I would be a moderate woman. My problem was that I judged things and people by my own yardstick. Once I got involved in things, I made it a rule to have them do like me. If it didn't go the way I intended, I got irritated and upset, and then angry at myself for not being able to be perfect. By the time I found out things were messed up, my husband would better stay out of my sight because I would take it out on him. I was a quite silly woman in the face of what I had done wrong. But that night, going in the wrong direction made me think once more how I had yet been strict towards myself. Considering that my mind seemed to be devastated by holding the strict rules for myself, I should try to be flexible to make my life easier and less stressful.

November 28, 2016

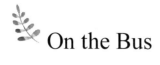 On the Bus

On the long seat of the two story sleeping bus I was looking out the window that seemed like featuring the panoramic green scenery of Vietnam. I was on the way to Mui Ne, a small town near the beach, after two-night stay in Ho Chi Minh. The scene of the landscape we passed through looked quite different from the one in the suburbs of Bangkok where I travelled a year earlier. Although travelling hadn't been my interest and I got used to enjoy a normal day evading any kind of adventure, the experience that I had in Thailand became the turning point to change my conception about the way of my life, and made me visit Ho Chi Minh and

Mui Ne.

Inside the bus which was equipped with twenty bunk beds lined in three columns, I could feel unusual and comfortable as well. All I had to do during the bus ride was to look out the window or look at some cell phone photos I took of the places and people. In Ho Chi Minh for three days everything was great except the drivers who conducted business with their vehicles at the airport. They tried to con me and my companions who seemed dopy because we weren't familiar with Veitnamese currency at all--that happening was too unpleasant to even mention. When we entered the city from the airport I was amazed by so many motorbikers who almost filled every street. They were riding in a horde side by side with other automobiles and bustled in and out of the buildings. Buses and cars honked horns to keep motorbikers from cutting in front of them or when they were approaching a crossing. Every street was filled with the sound of horns tooting. And every sidewalk was crowded with parked motorcycles that I mistook them for sale in a different dealership. The next day I found the sidewalk was a parking lot for motorcycles and there was a parking attendant for each shop, and pedestrians had to walk avoiding those motorbikes. On the first day it wasn't easy to adjust myself to that atmosphere. But that night I got accustomed to the surroundings enjoying a good meal with Vietnamese beer. Since the district we stayed was known to tourists so that we could bumped into them every step of the way, I could feel affinity for the city while I was walking down the street amid the big noise.

The next day we chose the War Memorial Museum of Vietnam first as one of several sightseeing spots for the tour around the city. At the gate I could feel some past things that would be sad. Each photo had historical meaning representing the sorrow of Vietnamese people. We could see they survived a long period of bitter Vietnam War and began a postwar reconstruction which they must be proud of. After the museum we headed to the Notredam Cathedral located a few blocks away on foot. We passed Reunification Palace and the nearby park along with hordes of motorbikers who were everywhere in the city because Vietnamese were riding motorcycles instead of automobiles. Unfortunately, the Cathedral was under construction, and we went into the famous Central Post Office. The Post Office was crowded with tourists who were taking pictures and browsing souvenir stores along with local people who visited to use postal services. The light yellow painted wall of the building with the long vaulted ceiling was impressive for me. As a tourist, I looked around the store located at the entrance to buy some souvenirs. Leaving the Post Office behind, we kept on walking under the hot sun to find a popular restaurant known to tourists and finally we were seated in the middle of the big old traditional one-story building next to a small artificial pond. It took time for us to select dishes from a thick volume of menu. After a big lunch, we went straight down Pasteur street and passed through the government office building to reach Dong Khoi, high end street. The Dong Khoi street was lined with shops and classy hotels and cafes.

It was nice to browse through each shop which was displaying various products. At a French door, wood frame with double glass, we peeped in at the door to have some coffee. Coffee was served in a small glass without the knob, but it was amazingly great. The deep savory taste made me feel that the place would grow on me. We all were content with what we'd done and seen that day while sipping coffee and looking over at foreigners walking in the street. At that moment I felt like I was in Buenos Aires where I once had lived--It had been called Paris in South America. For the rest of the day we walked around Dong Khoi street getting to know the town and then ended the day in a pub near our hotel. During the two days before we got on the bus for Mui Ne, we visited tourist attractions in Ho Chi Minh enjoying the city itself.

As I looked outside and inside the bus alternately glancing at other passengers who mostly closed eyes for a moment, only then did I find Vietnamese language looked like French from the signboards of the shops lined along the road. Since local people sounded Thai, I guessed Vietnamese words would be like Thai whose alphabet was very hard to be recognizable because of its curvilinear shape. But I was aware that Vietnamese can be learned on my own while I was looking at the countryside flashed past the bus window. Strange as it may sound, such a find was a kind of surprise and excitement. I had a hunch that I would try to become familiar with this language in the future.

At last six hour ride ended at the hotel we booked for two nights. Tall tropical trees with well kept gardens that I would happen to see on television welcomed us and we stepped into the passage to reach the hotel reception desk expecting an enjoyable experience.

December 16, 2016